JACK AND THE BEANSTALK

JACK AND THE BEANSTALK

Long ago, there lived a woman and her son, Jack, on a small farm. They were very poor. All they had was a cow.

"What shall we do?" asked Jack's mother, one day. "We don't have enough money to buy seeds for the farm this year! Go to the market and sell our cow. We shall get enough money to buy some seeds to plant a good crop."

"All right, mother," said Jack and went off to town.

He hadn't gone far when he met a funny old man. "Good morning, Jack," he said.

"Good morning to you," said Jack, wondering how the old man knew his name.

"Where are you going?" asked the man.

"I'm going to the market to sell our cow."

"Well, I have a special deal for you," said the man and opened his hand to show Jack what he held.

"Beans?" asked Jack, confused.

"These are magical seeds. If you plant them at night, they will grow up to the sky by morning," promised the old man. "The seeds are all yours in exchange for your old cow."

"Really?" said Jack.

"Yes! And if the beans don't work, you can have your cow back."

Jack exchanged the cow for the seeds and returned home. He told his mother how quickly he had sold their cow and got the magical seeds in return.

"What?" cried Jack's mother. "Oh, you silly boy! How could you give away our milking cow for three measly beans?"

Angrily, she threw the beans out of the window.

"How could I have been so foolish?" thought Jack . After much tossing and turning, at last, he drifted off to sleep.

When Jack woke up the next morning, he saw thick vines outside his window. He jumped out of bed, got dressed and ran to the garden. The beans his mother had thrown away had sprung up into a huge beanstalk which went up and up until it reached the sky!

Using the leaves and the vines, Jack climbed up the beanstalk until he reached the sky. When he got there, he found a tall castle. As he went inside, Jack heard a voice. "Fee, Fi, Fo, Fum!" Jack hid inside a cupboard and peeked out.

An enormous giant entered the room and sat down. On the table, there was a hen and a golden harp.

"Lay," said the giant and the hen laid a golden egg.

Then the giant growled, "Play," and the harp began to play a gentle tune. Then the giant began to sway his head and fell asleep.

Jack slowly crept out of the cupboard and grabbed the hen and the melodious harp. As he began to tiptoe back out, the hen cackled. This woke up the giant! He saw Jack and roared angrily, "Fee, Fi, Fo, Fum."

Jack ran as fast as he could and the giant rushed after him. Jack slipped and slid down the beanstalk as quickly as he could, with the angry giant at his heels.

As he was about to reach the bottom, Jack shouted, "Mother! Hurry! Please bring me an axe! Bring me an axe!"

His mother came rushing out to the garden with an axe in her hand. There, she stood still, frightened to see the enormous beanstalk.

Jack jumped down, got hold of the axe and quickly began to chop the beanstalk. The beanstalk toppled over. The giant fell down and broke his crown and no one ever saw him again.

Jack now had the hen that laid a golden egg every day. Jack used the money from selling the golden eggs to buy seeds for the crop. And so, Jack and his mother lived happily ever after.

Jack goes to sell his cow but he barters it for three beans instead. His mother is furious and throws the beans out of the window. The next morning, Jack sees giant beanstalks growing outside their house. Are the beans magical? Is he able to use them after all?

Om Books International

Reprinted in 2022

Corporate & Editorial Office
A-12, Sector 64, Noida 201 301,
Uttar Pradesh, India
Phone: +91 120 477 4100
Email: editorial@ombooks.com
Website: www.ombooksinternational.com

Sales Office
107, Ansari Road, Darya Ganj,
New Delhi 110 002, India
Phone: +91 11 4000 9000
Email: sales@ombooks.com
Website: www.ombooks.com

ISBN: 978-93-52760-13-8

Printed in India

10 9 8 7 6 5 4 3 2

eBOOK available

ISBN 978-93-5276-013-8 US $ 3.99 £ 2.99

www.ombooksinternational.com

0012500

Om KIDZ